For Leigh

Nutcracker Noel

Story by

Kate McMullan

Pictures by

Jim McMullan

Scholastic Inc.

New York   Toronto   London   Auckland   Sydney

ISBN 0-590-73901-8

Text copyright © 1993 by Kate McMullan.
Illustrations copyright © 1993 by Jim McMullan.
All rights reserved. Published by Scholastic Inc.,
555 Broadway, New York, NY 10012, by arrangement with
Michael di Capua Books / HarperCollins Publishers.

12 11 10 9 8 7 6 5 4 3 2   6 7 8 9/9 0 1/0

Printed in the U.S.A.   08

First Scholastic printing, November 1996

Noel dreamed of dancing in a real ballet.

So when Miss Olga swept into the studio one day,
saying that everybody was going to get
a part in *The Nutcracker*,
Noel believed her dream was coming true.

After class Miss Olga clapped for attention.
"This year, my assistant, Miss Crystal, will be
the Snow Queen. Nicky and Parker will be mice.
Elizabeth will be the marzipan doll and
Mia will be the gingerbread-cookie doll."
Miss Olga looked at her list.
"Noel will be a tree."

When she heard the news, Mia's mother
smothered Mia with kisses.
"My little cookie doll!" she exclaimed.

Noel felt sick to her stomach.

At the first rehearsal Noel counted seven
other trees. Not one of them was smiling.
Across the room the mice and dolls laughed
and played tag, using the piano for base.
Noel scampered over and got into the game.

When Miss Crystal asked the dolls to sit,
Noel sat right down.
"You're not a doll," Mia said loudly.
"Aren't you a tree?" said Miss Crystal.
"Nice try," said Parker as Noel trudged off.

Miss Olga handed out wooden spoons.
"Pretend these are candles," she said.
The trees *shu-shu-shushed* on tiptoe while
Miss Olga counted: "*One*-two-three! *Two*-two-three!"
Noel's feet began to hurt.
"Second-to-last tree," said Miss Olga.
"Stay with the counts."

Meanwhile, Miss Crystal showed the dolls how to twirl.
Mia twirled like a top.
She whirled like a tornado . . . and fell down.
"*Waaa!*" wailed Mia. "My ankle!"
Mia's mother burst through the door.
"Precious cookiekins!" she cried.

Noel cut out of line. "I'll take Mia's place!"

Mia hopped up. "Don't worry, everybody. I'm all right!"
"Parents out!" shouted Miss Olga.
"Second-to-last tree, back in line!"

After rehearsal Noel knocked
on Miss Olga's dressing-room door.
"Please, could you change me to a doll?"
"You think I'm a magician?" said Miss Olga.
"Ha! In my first ballet, I was a toadstool.
No one who saw me has ever forgotten
the way I fluttered my cap."

All the way home Noel tried to imagine
how it might feel to be green and prickly.

At dinner Noel refused her chair.
"I'm a tree," she said. "Trees don't sit."
"I hope trees eat broccoli," said her mother.

Noel fell asleep that night listening to
the tree-music tape Miss Olga had given her.
She dreamed she was deep in a forest.

Now, at rehearsals, Noel held her trunk straight
and stayed with the counts.
I am a tree, I am a tree, she thought.
My branches sway in the wind.

She tried never to look over at Mia,
who wouldn't stop twirling and whirling.

The Saturday before Christmas, everyone reported
to the theater. Dress rehearsal was at noon.
At eight o'clock the curtain would go up
for the opening night of *The Nutcracker*.
"Sorry," the stage-door guard told Mia's mother.
"Performers only."

Nicky and Parker were already in the costume room,
playing Go Fish in their mouse outfits.
Noel saw racks of doll dresses and
soldier uniforms, but no tree suits anywhere.

The guard appeared at the dressing-room door.
"Anybody here named Mia?"
"Me!" squealed Mia. "That's me!"

"Trees!" called Miss Olga. She led the way
to a rack of glittering gowns.
"What are these?" said Noel.
"Three guesses. Hands up, honey."
As Miss Olga slid on her costume, Noel turned
into a fir tree sprinkled with snow.

"Dolls!" called Miss Olga.
"Me first!" cried Mia. She stepped into
 the cookie-doll costume.
  Miss Olga zipped it up and put on the head.
"Wait a second." Mia's voice sounded far away.
"My mother won't even know it's *me* in here."
"That's show biz," said Miss Olga.

Dress rehearsal began.

Parker knocked over a reindeer.

The snow machine dumped out all the snow at once.

The Prince split his pants.

The littlest soldier threw up.

"The worse the rehearsal," declared Miss Olga,

"the better the show."

Noel found Mia sitting backstage by herself.
"You *are* a gingerbread cookie," Noel whispered.
"Believe it, and no one who sees you
 will ever forget your Christmas cookie dance."
"Dolls and mice!" called Miss Olga. "Places!"
 Mia put on her cookie-doll head.
"I *am* a cookie," came her faraway voice.

From the wings Noel peeked at the dolls
twirling and whirling. Mia danced deliciously.
As the orchestra struck up the tree music, a mist
rose from the forest floor, and Snow Queen Crystal
leaped onto the stage.
Miss Olga handed Noel her candle and . . .

the second-to-last tree *shu-shu-shushed* out
into the forest, adding her light to the night.

It wasn't exactly Noel's dream come true.

It was much, much better.